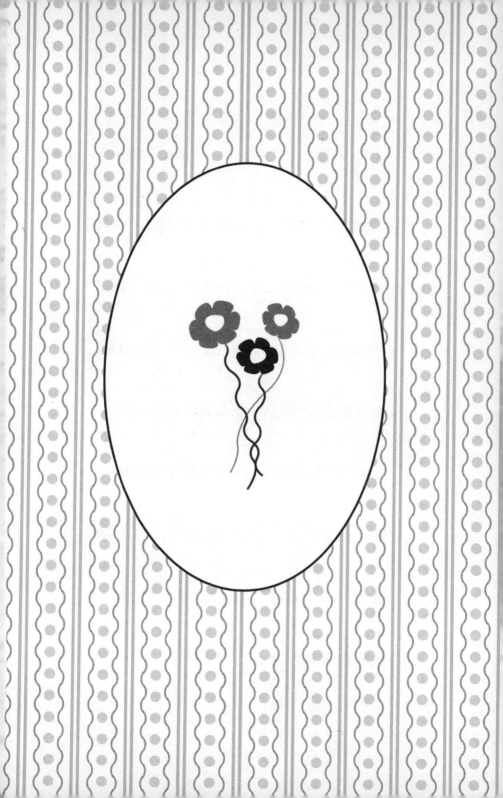

Enjoy all of the
Princess Posey, First Grader books

1
PRINCESS POSEY and the FIRST GRADE PARADE

2
PRINCESS POSEY and the PERFECT PRESENT

3
PRINCESS POSEY and the NEXT-DOOR DOG

4
PRINCESS POSEY and the MONSTER STEW

5
PRINCESS POSEY and the TINY TREASURE

6
PRINCESS POSEY and the NEW FIRST GRADER

7
PRINCESS POSEY and the CHRISTMAS MAGIC

8
PRINCESS POSEY and the FIRST GRADE BOYS

PRINCESS PSEY

and the

FIRST GRADE BOYS

Stephanie Greene

ILLUSTRATED BY

Stephanie Roth Sisson

G. P. PUTNAM'S SONS

AN IMPRINT OF PENGUIN GROUP (USA)

G. P. PUTNAM'S SONS
Published by the Penguin Group
Penguin Group (USA) LLC
375 Hudson Street
New York, NY 10014

USA | Canada | UK | Ireland | Australia
New Zealand | India | South Africa | China
penguin.com
A Penguin Random House Company

Library of Congress Cataloging-in-Publication Data
Greene, Stephanie.
Princess Posey and the first grade boys / Stephanie Greene ; illustrated by Stephanie
Roth Sisson.
pages cm
Summary: "Posey gets in trouble when she makes up a not-so-nice song about
one of the boys in her class"—Provided by publisher.
[1. Teasing—Fiction. 2. Behavior—Fiction. 3. Schools—Fiction.] I. Sisson, Stephanie
Roth, illustrator. II. Title.
PZ7.G8434Pnr 2014
[E]—dc23
2013020941

Printed in the United States of America.
ISBN 978-0-399-16364-7
1 3 5 7 9 10 8 6 4 2

Decorative graphics and design by Marikka Tamura.
Text set in Stempel Garamond.

For Jane

—S.G.

To Brian Getz,

Bellevue-Santa Fe Charter School's

gentle and wise principal.

—S.R.S.

CONTENTS

1 FIRST GRADE BOYS ARE SO ANNOYING 1

2 DANNY AND HIS STICKS 8

3 "POSEY'S COOL" 17

4 THE NOISE MONSTERS 24

5 A SILLY SONG 36

6 MEAN MISS LEE 42

7 NOT THE POSEY I KNOW 51

8 "MY STOMACH HURTS" 59

9 "YOU'LL MAKE HIM FEEL BAD!" 70

10 A ROCK WITH REAL DIAMONDS 79

FIRST GRADE BOYS ARE SO ANNOYING

It was writing time.

"Last week, we put words about nature on the Word Wall," Miss Lee told the class. "Today, I want you to use as many of them as you can in a story."

Posey loved to write stories. Today she would write one about a garden and put a beautiful fairy in it.

The room got quiet.

Then they all heard a rude noise.

"Miss Lee," someone said.

"It's Robert again."

"What do you say, Robert?"
said Miss Lee.

"Excuse me," Robert said.

The boys laughed.

The girls held their noses and
made faces.

"We're breathing poison air,"
Posey whispered.

Grace slapped her hands over her mouth and nose. Posey did, too.

Luca burped and fell off his chair.

"All right, class," Miss Lee called. "Calm down."

They always got silly when someone made a rude noise. It was hard to calm down.

"Posey and Grace? That's not necessary." Miss Lee sighed. "Luca, get back in your chair, please."

Some of the boys were still laughing.

"That's enough."
Miss Lee's voice
meant business.

The room got
quiet again.

Posey looked
at Ava, Nikki,
and Grace.

They made disgusted
faces at one another.
First grade boys
were so
annoying!

DANNY
AND HIS STICKS

After school, Posey's mom went to the dentist. Mrs. Romero came over to sit with Posey and Danny.

Posey did her homework at the table in the backyard. Danny pushed his truck over the grass.

First, he filled his truck with sticks. Then, he dumped them all out.

Then, he put them back in again, one at a time.

"It seems like a lot of work," said Mrs. Romero.

"Danny loves sticks," Posey said. "That's all he does, all day long."

She finished her work and put her paper in her backpack.

"Do you want to see how good I am at hopping?" she asked.

She hopped to the garage on one foot. She hopped back on her other foot.

"You're an excellent hopper," said Mrs. Romero.

Posey hopped around the sand-box.

"You're happy today," Mrs. Romero said. "How was school?"

"Good. But the boys were so annoying."

Posey told her about Robert. "Luca always burps and falls off his chair," she said.

"It's hard for some little boys to sit still," said Mrs. Romero.

"Miss Lee calls them jumping beans."

"I'm sure some of them are nice." Mrs. Romero smiled. "You might even have one as a friend someday."

"Not on your life!" said Posey. She sounded the way Gramps did when he said it.

Mrs. Romero laughed.

"POSEY'S COOL"

"Hey, Posey! Come here for a minute," someone yelled.

It was Tyler. He and Nick lived next door.

Tyler was in fourth grade. Nick was in second. They hardly ever asked Posey to come over.

"Can I?" Posey asked.

"Sure," said Mrs. Romero.

Posey ran across the driveway. Nick was sitting on their front steps. He had on a red hat.

Tyler was bouncing a basketball on the front walk.

"I want Nick to play, but he won't even talk to me," Tyler said.

"Why not?" said Posey.

"He won't talk to anyone," said

Tyler. "Go on. Say something to him."

"Hi, Nick," Posey said.

Nick didn't say anything.

"Ask him what day it is," Tyler said.

"What day is it?" Posey asked.

Nick didn't answer.

"I told you. He's weird." Tyler bounced the ball off the step near Nick's foot.

"Why won't he talk?" said Posey.

"He and his friend made up a new game," Tyler said. "The one who wears the red hat can't talk. The one who wears the green hat can. Ask him."

"What game are you playing?" said Posey.

Nick still didn't answer.

"Tell him he's a weirdo," said Tyler.

"You're a weirdo, Nick."

"See? Posey's cool."
Tyler held up his hand.
"Slap me five."

Posey slapped Tyler's hand. He dribbled the ball down the walk and through the front gate.

Posey was so proud. Tyler said she was cool!

She hopped all the way back to her own yard.

CHAPTER FOUR

THE NOISE
MONSTERS

The next morning, Miss Lee greeted Posey at the door to her classroom.

"I moved everyone around,"

Miss Lee said. "You need to find your name tag."

Miss Lee changed their seats every month. That way, they got to know everyone in the class.

Posey found her name at a table with Henry.

Henry was smart. He used big words. He bragged about his dad, who was a scientist.

A row of rocks was lined up on their table in front of him.

"You have to put your treasures in your cubby," Posey told him.

"They're not treasures. They're for a science experiment," said Henry.

"They're just dirty rocks."

"You will never be a scientist," Henry said.

"I will, too, if I want, Henry!" Posey said.

"Settle down, everyone," Miss Lee called. "It's time to do math problems."

She stopped at every table and put a piece of paper in front of each child.

When she got to Posey's table, Miss Lee told Henry to put his rocks in his cubby.

"I want you to take your time with these problems," Miss Lee told the class. "Some of you rushed last week and made mistakes."

Posey had made two mistakes. Today she wanted to get them all right. She wanted Miss Lee to say, "Great job!"

The first two problems were easy. The next problem was subtraction.

Subtraction was hard.

$$\begin{array}{r} 9 \\ -\ 3 \\ \hline \end{array}$$

Posey started to count on her fingers. Then she stopped.

"Miss Lee," Posey said. "Henry's humming."

"*Shhh*, Henry." Miss Lee held her finger to her lips.

"I like to hum. It helps me with my work," Henry said.

Miss Lee came over to their table. "It disturbs the other children," she told him.

"Fine." Henry put down his pencil. "I'm already finished."

"You are?" Miss Lee sounded

surprised. She looked at Henry's
paper. "Great job!" she said
quietly.

Posey frowned.

"At home I do third grade math with my father," Henry said.

"Be quiet!" said Posey.

"Posey . . . ?" Miss Lee said.

Posey went back to work. *No fair!* Henry was the one who was humming.

At recess, Posey said, "That Henry makes me so mad. He thinks he knows everything."

Posey, Ava, Nikki, and Grace had their arms around one another. It was fun to walk that way.

They could tell secrets and no one could hear.

"I wish he wasn't at my table," Posey said.

"Nate's at my table," said Nikki. "He taps his pencil all day long."

The boys in their class were playing tag. They shouted and ran

around. They pulled one another's jackets and rolled on the ground.

"Boys are so noisy," said Grace.

Luca ran up to them and stuck out his tongue. "Na-nah, boo-boo, you can't catch me!" he shouted.

"We could if we wanted, Luca!" Posey shouted back.

"Slowpokes! Slowpokes!" the other boys yelled.

"You're pains in the neck! You're pains in the neck!" Ava shouted.

"Boys make me so mad!" Posey said. "Come on! We have to get away from the noise monsters!"

CHAPTER
FIVE

A SILLY SONG

The girls ran across the play-ground. They passed Henry. He was kneeling near the fence.

"Watch out! It's the rock monster!" Posey screamed.

Nikki, Ava, and Grace screamed, too. It was so exciting to pretend. It felt like they were running away from real monsters.

They didn't stop until they got to the swings.

"My heart feels like it's going to jump out of my body," Nikki panted.

"I never ran so fast in my whole life," said Ava.

"Why does Henry like rocks so much?" Grace asked.

"Because he's weird." Posey remembered what Tyler had said. "He's a weirdo."

Her friends giggled.

"Henry is a weirdo," Posey said. "He has a beard-o."

"Boys can't have beards," Nikki said.

"My uncle has a bushy beard that goes up to his ears." Ava giggled.

"Henry's goes down to his belly button!" Posey said.

"Posey!" Grace cried.

Nikki and Ava laughed so hard.

"Henry is a weirdo. He has a beard-o," Posey sang. She swung her arms. She stamped her feet. "Come on. Let's do a parade!"

Ava and Nikki and Grace joined her.

"*Henry is a weirdo.*
He has a beard-o,"
they all sang. The
words felt so silly.
The more they sang,
the sillier it felt.
"*Henry is a weirdo,*"
they sang as loud as they
could. "*He has a—*"
"Stop that this minute!"
called a sharp voice.

MEAN MISS LEE

The parade stopped.

It was Miss Lee. She looked angry.

"What do you think you are doing?" she asked.

Posey looked at the ground.
They had been having so much fun.
Now she felt embarrassed.

There was a silence.

"Well? I'm waiting,"
Miss Lee said.

"Posey started it,"
Grace said in a small
voice.

"She made up a song,"
Ava whispered.

"Posey, is that true?"
Miss Lee's voice was cold.
Posey didn't know where to look.
She didn't know how to stand.

She pinched the edge of her skirt and held on tight.

"Posey . . . ?"

Posey didn't want to look Miss Lee in the eye. Miss Lee's face scared her.

"Look at me, please," Miss Lee said.

Posey squinted her eyes when she looked up so Miss Lee wouldn't know how she felt.

"What were you thinking?" Miss Lee said.

Posey's mouth felt stiff. "It was a game," she said.

"Do you think Henry enjoyed your game?"

Posey looked at Henry. He was watching them. His arms hung at his sides.

Posey looked back at the ground.

"I'm disappointed in you," said Miss Lee. "It's not a game when you gang up on someone and call them names. It's being a bully."

Posey's eyes opened wide.

Posey, a *bully*? How could Miss Lee say that? Bullies were bad. Posey was a nice girl.

"You hurt Henry's feelings," Miss Lee said. "You will have to work this out with him."

Posey didn't want to work out anything.

She wasn't a bully. Miss Lee was mean.

"You're good at working things out, and I'm sure you're sorry," said Miss Lee.

Posey wasn't sorry.

She was mad.

Miss Lee was mean to call her a bully. She was mean to make them feel bad about their fun game, too.

Posey would never like Miss Lee again.

NOT THE POSEY
I KNOW

Posey didn't tell Gramps about it when he picked her up after school. She wasn't going to tell her mom, either.

But when her mom came home, she already knew. She came up

the stairs and stopped in Posey's doorway.

Posey usually put on her pink tutu after school. Today, she had spread it out in a circle on her bed. Her stuffed animals were sitting around the edge. She was curled up tight in the middle.

"Posey, sit up, please," her mom said.

Posey sat up. She crossed her arms over her chest.

"I got an e-mail from Miss Lee this afternoon," said her mom. "What she told me didn't sound like the Posey I know."

"Miss Lee's mean." Posey stuck out her lower lip.

"No, Miss Lee is concerned." Her mom sat on the edge of the bed. "She knows you're a nice girl. But you ganged up on another child and hurt his feelings."

"We were playing a fun game," Posey said.

"It might have been fun for you. It wasn't for Henry," her mom said. "You know it's not nice to call people names."

"Tyler did. He called Nick a weirdo."

"I don't know about Tyler and Nick. But that's not a nice thing to call someone," her mom said. "Especially when a group does it. Imagine how Henry felt."

Posey didn't want to imagine about Henry.

"I'm sure you didn't mean to hurt his feelings. But you know in your heart that what you did wasn't kind."

"No, I don't," Posey said stubbornly.

"Then you need to think about it some more."

Her mom went downstairs. Posey curled into a ball again. She held Roger the giraffe tight against her and squeezed her eyes shut.

Her mom didn't care that Miss Lee hurt Posey's feelings when she called her a bully.

No one did.

They all just cared about Henry.

Posey didn't feel sorry for him.

She only felt sorry for herself.

CHAPTER EIGHT

"MY STOMACH HURTS"

"Posey, breakfast!" her mom called the next morning.

Posey went down to the kitchen.

"Why aren't you dressed?" her mom said when she saw Posey's pajamas.

"My stomach hurts."

"Go back up and get dressed." Her mom put a bowl on the tray of Danny's high chair. She opened the refrigerator door. "You'll feel better after you eat."

"My face hurts, too."

"We don't have time for this today," her mom said. "I have an early meeting. Gramps is taking you to school. Now hurry."

Ava and Nikki and Grace were waiting for Posey near her cubby.

"Miss Lee said Henry has a

stomachache," Ava said in a scared voice.

"My mom said I have to say sorry," said Nikki.

"Me, too," said Grace.

Posey didn't want to talk about it. She went to her table and sat down. Henry's place was empty.

She sat by herself all day long.

❀ ❀ ❀

Gramps picked Posey up after
school. "How was your day?" he
asked.

"Bad."

Gramps drove in silence for a
while.

"Life sure is a funny thing," he said finally. "One day, you can feel like the happiest person in the world. The next, it's like there's a storm cloud hanging over your head."

Posey didn't say anything.

"Your cloud looks like a real humdinger," Gramps teased. "I should have brought my umbrella."

Posey didn't smile.

"Who are you mad at?" Gramps asked.

"Everyone."

"That's a lot of people." Gramps turned into the driveway. "Maybe you should figure out where it all started and take it from there."

Posey went up to her bedroom without having a snack.

"Danny and I are going out-side," Gramps called up the stairs. "Are you coming?"

"No," said Posey.

"I'll be outside if you need me."

Posey heard the kitchen door close. Then she heard laughing outside. She pressed her face against the window.

Mrs. Romero and Gramps were helping Danny find sticks. They looked like they were having fun.

Posey put on her pink tutu and her veil.

Who cares if everyone was mean to her? She was Princess Posey. She could go anywhere and do anything.

All by herself.

Posey went and stood in front of her mirror.

"Miss Lee was mean to me," she said.

Princess Posey looked
back at her.

"Henry acts as if he knows everything," Posey said.

Princess Posey didn't say a word.

"Well, he does." Posey's shoulders sagged. "Everyone's being mean to me."

Princess Posey's eyes were steady and calm. *She* knew where the whole thing had started.

So did Posey.

"YOU'LL MAKE HIM FEEL BAD!"

Gramps was sitting alone when Posey got outside.

"Where's Mrs. Romero?" she asked.

"She had to go shopping."
Gramps stood up. "Stay with
Danny while I run in and get him
something to drink. I'll be right
out."

"Okay."

Posey sat on her swing. Tyler
and another boy rode up the driveway on their bikes. They stopped
in front of Tyler's garage.

"What's that kid doing?" the
boy said.

"He's playing," said Posey.

"He just dumped the sticks out.
Why's he putting them back?"

"Because he likes to," Posey said.

"What a weirdo," the boy said. He laughed.

"Yeah, Danny is a little weirdo," said Tyler. He laughed, too.

"He is not a weirdo, you big bullies!" Posey jumped off her swing and raced toward them.

"You'll hurt his feelings if you call him names!" she shouted. "You'll make him feel bad!"

Tyler put out his hands to stop her.

"Hey, Posey, we're only kidding," Tyler said. "Marcos is sorry. Tell her, Marcos."

"Sorry," said Marcos. "I think he's cool. I collected dead worms when I was little."

"You say it now," Posey told Tyler.

"Sorry, Danny." Tyler picked up a stick and held it out. "Here you go. Another one for your collection."

Danny threw his arms around Tyler's leg.

"See? Danny and I are friends." Tyler ruffled Danny's hair. "I won't call him names anymore, okay?"

"You better not."

Posey gave Danny a fierce hug when the boys left.

They had made fun of him the same way she made fun of Henry.

It was her turn to say sorry.

A ROCK
WITH
REAL DIAMONDS

Henry was at their table when Posey got to school in the morning.

"I'm sorry I called you a name," she said.

Henry was arranging his rocks. He didn't look up.

"You just love rocks, don't you?" said Posey.

Henry nodded.

"That's like my brother, Danny. He loves sticks." Posey put something on the table. "You can have this for your collection. It has real diamonds in it."

It was a sparkly rock.

Posey had found it on a nature walk. She pretended it was

the treasure the magic unicorn
had to guard when she played her
Magic Land game.

"It isn't diamonds," Henry said.
"It's mica."

"What's mica?"

"It's a mineral found in rocks," said Henry. "I'm going to be a geologist when I grow up. They study rocks."

"Maybe Danny will be a scientist, too," Posey said. "I'm going to be a dog trainer."

"Dogs are noisy," Henry said. "They also bite."

"Hero never bites," Posey said. "He lives next door to me. You could come over and meet him."

"What if he doesn't like me?"

"He will if you're my friend."

"I can help your brother look for sticks," said Henry.

"Okay. You ask your mom and I'll ask mine."

Posey went to put her things in her cubby. She stopped at Miss Lee's desk on the way.

"Henry knows everything about rocks," Posey said. Then she whispered, "But he's afraid of dogs."

"He is?" Miss Lee whispered back.

Posey nodded. "I asked him to my house to meet Hero."

"I'm glad you worked things out."

Posey gave a small hop. "I'm good at working things out, aren't I?"

"Yes, you are." Miss Lee smiled. "And you always feel better after you do."

"I know."

Happiness bubbled up in Posey like a fountain. She twirled around. "Life sure is a funny thing, isn't it, Miss Lee?" she said.

Miss Lee laughed. "It sure is, Posey," she said. "It sure is."

Watch for the next **PRINCESS POSEY** book!

PRINCESS POSEY
and the
VALENTINE'S DAY BALLET

Valentine's Day is coming! Posey is so excited about her special ballet recital and giving cards to everyone at school. Then she learns that one of her classmates doesn't have any valentines to give out. Can Princess Posey and her tutu find the perfect way to help?

12-14